Little Big Sister

Written by

Amy B. McCoy

Illustrations by

Adriana Tonello

Library of Congress Cataloging-in-Publication Data

McCoy, Amy B.

Little Big Sister / by Amy B. McCoy

p. cm.

Summary: Nine-year-old Katie describes her life as a younger sibling to an
older brother who has autism and other disabilities. She faces unique
challenges and makes a difference at her school.

ISBN 978-0692651414

[1. Siblings – Fiction. 2. Family – Fiction. 3. Disabilities – Fiction.
4. Autism – Fiction. 5. Interpersonal Relationships – Fiction.] 1. Title

Printed in the United States of America

Dedicated to Greg, Matthew, and Kathryn,

with so much love.

Chapter One

Hoping

"Mom, I need you!" I called from my bedroom. I was sitting at my desk, making a new list in my favorite notebook.

"I'll be there in a minute, Katie," she replied.

When Mom says, "in a minute," it feels like an hour before she even comes to see what I need. Mom is always with Michael, my brother. He is eleven and has autism. And ADHD. And apraxia (a speech disorder). He needs Mom *all* the time. He can't even use the bathroom or get dressed alone. I am nine, and they expect me to do *everything* on my own.

"Mom! Now!" I mean, really, do I have to break a bone to get some attention around here?

"OK, honey, I'm just getting Mikey settled," I heard her call out to me from my brother's room. She was using her "trying to stay calm" voice which meant she was frustrated over whatever Michael was doing.

Everyone who meets Michael loves him because he is so smiley and friendly. He talks to everyone he meets. He has full conversations with people he doesn't even know in the grocery store and at the library. Dad says it's like he is the mayor of our town. Wherever we go, people know him and they are always so happy to see him. But they don't have to live with him. They don't see him rolling around on the floor kicking and screaming when the smallest thing doesn't go his way. They don't know how hard it is to be his sister.

As I waited for Mom, I looked out the window by my desk and noticed the snow had almost all melted. It was late in the afternoon on a Thursday at the end of March. We had a half day of school today because the teachers had a meeting. I love it when school ends early! A few teenagers were playing basketball across the street. We don't have any kids my age on our street, just a bunch of teenagers. I saw a huge truck driving down our street. That should get Michael's attention. He calls himself "the Neighborhood Watch" because he loves looking out his window, keeping watch over the neighborhood. He keeps track of what time all the neighbors leave for work in the mornings and what time they arrive back home in the evenings. Maybe now that there was this enormous truck for Michael to watch, he would be occupied long enough for Mom to remember that I exist. Yup, she knocked on my door.

"Hi, Katie, did you need me?" Mom asked.

YES, I need you. You're my Mom, but you are never around when I call for you, I thought to myself, but of course I didn't say it out loud. "Yes." I concentrated on making my voice sound kind and pleasant. "Can we please go to the mall today? I really need some new clothes."

"Well, not today, Katie. I don't have anyone to watch Michael, and it's already late," Mom said. "Let's make a plan to go to the mall this weekend, when Dad can watch Mikey."

"OK," I replied, hoping she wouldn't forget.

Mall List

Spring Tops
Sandals and flip flops
Shorts
Bathing Suit (maybe)

Chapter Two

Dinner and Hoops

That night, dinner was louder than usual. Michael was upset because our school day was shortened. He loves routines, and when his schedule is just a bit different from usual, he has lots of meltdowns. AND HE IS LOUD. Mom says he is getting better about understanding when routines and schedules have to be changed. She calls it *"learning to be flexible,"* but I don't see any improvement. Michael was repeating, "School ends at three thirty on Friday. Right, Mommy?" over and over all throughout our dinner. I know he was just making sure he would be back to his regular routine tomorrow, but Dad said that he sounded like a broken record. That's Dad's old-fashioned way of letting us know Michael says the same thing over and over. I wish we could have quiet family dinners with typical conversations, but Michael makes that impossible.

Mom kept saying, "Yes, Mikey, you have a regular day of school till three thirty tomorrow," but it wasn't enough for him. He had to ask it louder and louder till finally, Dad wrote it out on paper for him so he could just read the answer. That quieted him down for a little while. Here's what Dad's note said:

Michael has a regular day of
school on Friday, March 23.

Michael will be at school
until 3:30 just like usual.

So, that's one good thing about Michael: he is a good reader.

As we were finishing up dinner, I asked Dad if he wanted to play basketball in the driveway after I helped out with the dishes. Dad loves when I offer to help with chores around the house like washing and drying dishes, and he also loves sports. So I figured I would help with the dinner cleanup, play some hoops, and then ask him about hanging out with Michael on Saturday while Mom takes me to the mall. Good strategy, huh?

"So, Dad," I began as I dried the pots and pans he'd washed. "I want to go to the mall with Mom, and she said she could take me on Saturday. Can you watch Michael so we can go?"

"Oh, great," Dad replied. "I need a few things for work at the mall, too. Why don't we all go as a family?"

My heart sank. I really wanted to go to the mall with just Mom; I didn't want Michael to be there. He makes mall trips stressful, and we always end up leaving before I've barely started shopping.

"OK…sounds good," I replied quietly, but I didn't really mean it. I know Dad is always trying to find ways for us to spend time together as a family. But I don't think he remembers the time we tried to go to the movies last month and we ended up leaving the theater while they were still playing the previews. The actual movie hadn't even started yet! Michael kept yelling, "Too dark! Too dark! Too dark!" Plus, he was constantly asking, "Where is Buzz Lightyear?" I guess he thought going to the movies meant seeing Buzz Lightyear on the big screen, since the *Toy Story* movies are the only movies he will watch at home. We had to leave. It was *beyond* embarrassing. At least I didn't see anyone there that I knew.

After we put the last of the pots and pans away, Dad and I went outside to play basketball in the driveway. Just as I was starting to get a few baskets in a row, Michael came out. He saw me shoot the ball and he clapped for me. "Good job, Katie! Good job, Katie! Good job, Katie!" he said three times with a huge smile. That's another good thing about

Michael. He always cheers people on, even if they don't want to be cheered on, like me.

"Katie, let Michael have a turn," Dad said.

I bounced the ball to him. Of course he didn't catch it, and the ball rolled under Mom's car. *Oh well, game over.*

Dad rescued the ball, handed it to Michael, and lowered the basketball hoop as low as it would go. Michael tried and tried to make a basket, and on what seemed like his twenty-fifth try, he finally got the ball in the basket. He never gives up.

Go Mikey!

What Made Me Smile Today

Having a short day of school

Playing basketball with Dad

When Mikey made a basket after dinner

Chapter Three

Wondering and Wishing

The next morning was like any other morning. I was in my room, getting dressed and ready for school. All of a sudden, my door flew open and in barged Michael. He was holding Pepper, my favorite stuffed animal, the soft bunny I've had since I was born! The one I still sleep with (even though I know I'm too old to sleep with a stuffed animal). He said, "Look, Katie, I have Pepper!" in his teasing voice.

The next thing I knew, Pepper went into his mouth. I watched as Michael licked and bit him.

"AAHHHH!" I screamed, "Mom! Michael bit Pepper!"

Mom was already running up the stairs. She quietly took Pepper from Michael, made him apologize, and put him in time out. Then she tried to hand Pepper back to me.

"No, Mom! I'm not touching Pepper till it's washed. Gross! He has Mikey's germs and is all wet and *disgusting* from his spit!"

"OK, honey, I'll wash Pepper while you're at school." Mom added Pepper to the laundry basket at the top of the stairs.

All we could hear was Michael in his room, happily shrieking to himself, "Happy Friday! Happy Friday! Happy Friday!" I don't know anyone like him who is so happy about the days of the week and happy to be in time out. He just doesn't make sense to me. I hope Mom never lets him out of time out. At the same time, I wonder what it would feel like to be Michael. To feel that happy about the day changing from Thursday to Friday. Don't get me wrong, I love

Fridays too, since they start off the weekend. I just can't imagine jumping up and down about it.

I wish I had a brother who would actually play with me. All Michael likes to do is pull garbage cans around in the driveway and watch our neighbors drive their cars from his window. Oh yes, he also likes to ruin my things. Once, last year, I brought home a special gift for Mom that I made at school for Mother's Day. I hid the gift in one of Dad's drawers, and Michael found it and opened it. I was SO MAD! Luckily, my dad was able to fix it. Michael ruins everything. I have to lock my room and hide all of my stuff. Mom has to lock up her computer, the TV remotes, and all the electronics in the house.

No one knows what it's like for me. What it's like to have this brother who is so annoying. I know other kids have siblings who irritate them. Big brothers who wrestle them or little sisters who copy them all the time. It's different for me. My brother is a big brother who acts like a little brother. Even though he is older than me, he seems a lot younger. He watches little-kid TV shows even though he is eleven years old. He reads preschool books, too. It's embarrassing for me when my friends come over because some of them laugh at him when he makes his weird noises. Oh, did I mention the weird noises? He sounds like he's singing (but he's not) in a very excited, high-pitched voice. Also, and this is *really* embarrassing, when he has to go to the bathroom, he pulls down his pants BEFORE he gets to the bathroom (so everyone sees his backside as he runs with his pants down around his knees to the bathroom). He never remembers to close the door, so we all hear him doing his business while he's in there. And just in case you were wondering, no, he doesn't remember to flush or to wash his hands after he pees either. Mom always has to remind him.

Flapping his hands is another embarrassing thing Michael does. Mom says that lots of kids with autism flap. His hands do a small, flapping motion like a bird, but in front of his body. The flapping mostly happens when he is excited or happy. The way I have heard Mom describe it to other kids is, *"Imagine he is smiling with his whole body. Flapping is his way of telling us he is happy and smiling on the inside."* But I know most kids don't really get it about flapping, and I hate seeing kids make fun of him when he flaps.

Sometimes, I wish I had a younger sister. It's lonely with just Michael around since he doesn't know how to play with me. If I had a younger sister, I could teach her so many things! But Mom says she is too old to have any more babies.

I want someone to ride bikes with me, play board games, build Legos—you know, all the stuff a brother or sister does with you when you're bored. Michael can't ride a bike. Mom says that is too much coordination and balance for him. He has a bike, but with training wheels, and he still needs lots of help with it. The only board game he likes to play is Sorry, and that gets old after a while. And he is hopeless at Legos. He only likes to pull out garbage cans and watch our neighbors from his window. Boring, if you ask me.

<u>Wishes</u>

To have a little sister

Mikey didn't have autism

Mikey would stop flapping

For Mikey to play with me

Chapter Four

Bella

I like my school because it's one of the newer schools in our town. One of the things I love about my school is that it has air conditioning. Another thing I love about my school is that the older kids (like me) get our own lockers. We don't have to share lockers anymore like we did in kindergarten, first, and second grades. Also, the third grade classrooms are upstairs with the fourth and fifth graders. I like being upstairs away from the little kids.

Our teacher, Mrs. Magee, is really kind. She

never yells, and she knows how to make me feel comfortable in her classroom. I guess you could say that I am one of those kids who worries a lot. Mrs. Magee helps me feel less worried about school. If I don't understand something, I know I can ask her and she will help me. And I like how she calls me up to her desk when she is helping me instead of explaining something just to me at my desk in front of the entire class. She gives us candy on Fridays! When she catches her students really focused on their work in class or when we do a great job on homework, she gives us raffle tickets. We write our name on the tickets and put them in Mrs. Magee's raffle jar. Then on Fridays, she shakes up the tickets in the jar and pulls out about fifteen tickets so lots of kids can win candy. The more times your name is in the raffle jar, the more chances you have to win. A few Fridays ago, my name was picked five times! I got a lot of candy that day and some other small prizes, too. I guess that was my lucky day!

Each week, we get a new classroom job. Sometimes I am the line leader, sometimes I am the paper passer and sometimes I am the chair helper (not a fun job). Of all the classroom jobs, my favorite one is the elevator helper. My friend, Bella, was born with legs that are not very strong. She uses a walker to get around school. Going up and down stairs is hard for her, so she has to use the elevator. See, I told you our school is cool—it even has an elevator! When Bella was born, the doctors told her parents that she might never be able to walk. Well, they were wrong! She can walk; she just needs her walker if it's a long walk.

Bella has a disability, but I don't know what it's called. Her disability is so different from Michael's, though. He is grabby and not very much fun for me to be around. Bella is gentle and fun to be with. She is also really brave. Last month in the school talent show, when most kids got up on the stage to do dances, gymnastics or play a musical instrument, Bella went on the school stage with a microphone and read a poem she wrote about having hope. I saw Mom wipe her eyes while listening to Bella read her poem. She called them "happy tears."

Anyway, I love when it's my turn to be the elevator helper because that means I get to spend more time with Bella. Since our specials like art, music, library, and gym are all on the first floor, she uses the elevator when we go to them and to lunch. I think she might be the only student who uses it, besides the fifth grader who is on crutches right now for a broken leg. I know there is a boy in kindergarten who uses a wheelchair. When he becomes a third grader, he will have to use the elevator to get to his classroom, too.

When I got to school Friday morning, Bella was already there with a huge smile. She pointed to the job chart that showed my turn as elevator helper was coming soon!

I smiled back at her. "Hi, Bella, how was your half day off from school yesterday?"

"It was great!" said Bella. "I went to the mall!"

"Lucky! What did you get?" I asked.

"I got something good!" replied Bella.

"What was it? Something from Polka Dots?" I

asked. Polka Dots is our favorite store.

"No, even better than that," she said. "I walked around the inside of the mall two times without my walker!"

"Wow, Bella, that *is* something awesome!" I told her.

"I've been practicing and practicing. I used to only be able to walk past a few stores before needing my walker. But yesterday I walked the entire loop! Then I did it again! My dad couldn't believe it. He took lots of pictures and videos of me!" Bella was so excited.

Have I mentioned how just being around Bella makes me smile?

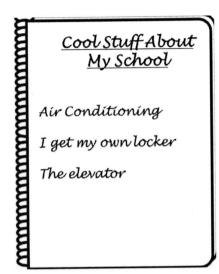

Cool Stuff About My School

Air Conditioning

I get my own locker

The elevator

Chapter Five

Not-So-Exciting News

"Good morning," said Mrs. Magee on Friday morning at school. "I have some exciting news to share before we start our day!"

Whenever teachers say something like, "exciting news," it's not really that exciting. I mean, "exciting" is a trip to Disney World. I hoped she wasn't going to tell us the school got new computers or something like that. That is so *not* exciting to me.

"We are going to welcome a new student to

our class next week. His name is Adam, and he just moved to Connecticut from Ohio," she announced.

So the "exciting news" is a new student joining our class, and it's a boy? Not that exciting at all. See, I told you.

"Today, Mrs. Peters is going to have a meeting with our class to tell us a little bit about Adam," she continued. Mrs. Peters is our school guidance counselor. Sometimes I talk to her when I have worried thoughts. My mom and Mrs. Peters call it "anxiety," but that's just a fancy word that means being worried. Like I said, I am a worrier.

Olivia raised her hand: she was always trying to be the first one with her hand up. "Why is Mrs. Peters coming?" she asked. *Good question,* I thought to myself. I mean, I like when Mrs. Peters comes to talk to us, but I was curious about why she was coming to tell us about the new kid. What's his name again? Oh yeah, Adam.

"Well..." Mrs. Magee looked a little uncomfortable, like she didn't know how to answer the question. "She just wants to tell us about Adam because he has some special needs."

"Me too!" Bella chimed in with her huge smile. "Maybe Adam can sit next to me, Mrs. Magee. We already have something in common!"

"Maybe," said Mrs. Magee. "Oh look, here she is now! Hello, Mrs. Peters." She looked relieved that Mrs. Peters had arrived.

"Hi, everyone!" Mrs. Peters smiled. "Time to stand up and stretch your hands up to the ceiling. Now, bend at your waist to touch your toes. Move your hands forward on the floor, away from your feet. You are in downward dog pose." Mrs. Peters always begins her meetings with some yoga poses.

"Woof woof," some of the boys said as soon as they heard the word "dog." The boys in my class can be so immature, but I always laugh when they bark during the downward dog pose.

"Come sit on the floor at the front of the room with me," said Mrs. Peters to the class after she led us through two more yoga poses. "So Mrs. Magee told you a new student is joining your class next week?"

"Yes," we all replied together.

"I wanted to have this meeting to tell you a bit about Adam. He may seem a little different to you at first. Adam is nonverbal. Does anyone know what that means?"

I was pretty sure nonverbal meant that he couldn't talk, but I didn't want to raise my hand.

Olivia's hand shot up first again. "Does it mean something like nouns and verbs?"

"Nice try, Olivia, but no, it does not," said Mrs. Peters. "Anyone else?"

Timmy had his hand up too. He was always raising his hand, just like Olivia. Even when they don't know the answers, those two always have their hands up.

But Mrs. Peters didn't call on Timmy. She looked right at me. Did she know that I knew the answer? I sort of moved my hand. I almost wanted to answer her question, but I couldn't force myself to really raise my hand. Mrs. Peters called on me anyway. "Katie? What do you think nonverbal means?"

"Um, does it mean that he can't talk with words?" I asked quietly.

"Yes. Good job, Katie," she said. I smiled. I do love getting answers right. Mrs. Peters continued, "Adam can read, he can write, and he can understand everything you say. He can say what he wants back to you using a tablet. Like Katie said, he just doesn't talk with words."

Then, I sort of spaced out a little. I stopped listening to Mrs. Peters and started thinking about Michael. Mom says he couldn't talk until he was five years old and that she and Dad were told by some doctors that he might never talk. Well, those doctors were wrong. He does talk now, and he never stops.

As I tuned back in to the lesson, Mrs. Peters was talking about how Adam needs a lot of help and will have a teacher's aide with him all the time. Then she asked if any of us had any questions. Of course,

Timmy and Olivia were the first with their hands up. "So what is *wrong* with him?" asked Timmy.

This question always makes me so mad. I hate it when people ask me what is wrong with Michael. It's just so mean and rude.

Mrs. Peters stared at Timmy for a few seconds while she tried to think of an answer. "He was born that way." That was her response. I totally wished I had the courage to raise my hand at that moment. I knew I could explain it better than that. I know exactly what it's like to live with someone who has autism. That's what Mrs. Peters was describing about Adam, but without using the word autism. I had so many thoughts running through my head. My face was getting red from just thinking about raising my hand to answer Timmy's annoying question. But I kept my hand in my lap.

Bella quickly raised her hand and explained, "Just like I was born with legs that aren't very strong, Timmy. I can still walk with my walker, and I'm also learning to walk without my walker. Maybe one day Adam will talk with words. We have to give him a chance." Somehow, Bella always has such kind things to say. Even though she's only nine, like me, she knows how to sound so grown up when she talks.

Then, before I knew it, Mrs. Peters stood up and said, "That's it for today. If anyone has any questions, you know where to find me." Then she winked at me and walked over to where Bella and I were sitting, reminding us that we have lunch bunch with her on Monday. Lunch bunch is when we eat lunch in Mrs. Peters's office once a week instead of the loud cafeteria. We play games with a small group of other girls. It's fun!

Questions I Hate

So, what is wrong with your brother?

Why does he flap his hands like that?

Why does your brother watch baby shows on TV?

Chapter Six

The Mall

"No, Michael! STOP!" I screamed. My brother decided to suddenly jump off the seesaw that we were on together at the playground after school on Friday. THUD, I came crashing down as he ran off. Ouch, that really knocked the wind out of me.

"Are you OK, Katie?" my mom paused to ask me. I was trying to catch my breath, but she didn't even wait for my reply because she was running off to make sure Michael didn't dart into the parking lot. He ran to the monkey bars this time. That's where she found him. Not the parking lot. He was trying to cross the monkey bars but not waiting his turn, as usual. I was on the ground. My backside really hurt from the seesaw crash. Even though I knew he didn't mean to hurt me, my whole body was tense, and I was so embarrassed I had tears in my eyes. Why did he have to be such a pain?

And really, who wants to be at the playground? The playground is for little kids. I want to be at the mall, but no, we had to come here because Michael wanted to play at the playground and Mom said we all needed fresh air after being stuck inside all winter. I don't care about fresh air. I just want to get some new clothes at the mall. Even though we had a plan to go to the mall tomorrow, I just couldn't wait and wanted to go today instead.

"Please, Mom," I begged, "can't we go to the mall today?"

"Well…" I could hear the consideration in her voice. "Michael will be in a good mood when we are done here at the playground after all this fresh air. So, let's give it a try and go straight from here." I could hear a hint of doubt in her tone.

"*What*? With *him*?" I asked. I was hoping she would get a sitter to stay home with him.

"Yes, Katie. Your brother is perfectly capable of going to a few stores at the mall today," she replied quickly.

Sometimes I think she forgets who he is. He is *not* capable of going to the mall, today or ever. But if that's the only way to get some new spring clothes today, I'll take it.

So, off we went to the mall. I was trying my best to be hopeful that Michael would not be embarrassing or make a scene while we were there. I had a feeling that something would go wrong, but I tried to ignore that feeling as I focused on all the cute spring shirts, shorts, and shoes I was hopefully going to bring home.

At the first store—Polka Dots, of course—I picked out a few things that were on my list. I was ready for Mom to buy them, but she said, "No, you have to try the clothes on and make sure they fit." So I went in the dressing room alone since Mom had to watch Michael. He was looking at the backpacks and journals with initials on them, counting all the ones that had the letter M. At least the counting was keeping him quiet. I liked the clothes I tried on, and they fit! While Mom went to go wait in line to pay, she asked me if I would look at the backpacks with Michael. I had to say OK; after all, she was about to buy me some cool new clothes. So I stood with Michael and pretended to be interested in the backpacks. We counted all the ones with the letters M and K on them. He found twenty-two total items with M and K on them and was so happy with himself since he always says twenty-two is his favorite number. He started jumping and flapping and happily screeching, "Twenty-two, Katie, twenty-two! That's my favorite number!" People were staring. It was so embarrassing, and I just froze. Luckily, at that very moment, Mom had finished paying. She walked over to us, took Michael by the hand, and led us out of the store.

I followed closely behind Mom and Michael. As they turned to walk toward the mall exit, Michael noticed the computer store. He loves the computer store. He knows how to work all the computers and tablets, and they actually allow customers to touch everything in there. He started running for the computer store, and Mom had to quickly chase after him. Then I had to start running too, just to keep up. I didn't want to get lost in the mall! Mom set the timer on her phone for five minutes and told Michael, "OK, you can look around for five minutes, and then we have to go." She gave him the four-minute warning, the three-minute warning, the two-minute warning and of course, the one-minute warning. The timer on her phone went off, and she told him, "OK, Mikey, it's time to go."

He wouldn't listen. He wouldn't move. He turned his body into a heavy blob on the floor, impossible to pick up. "That was fun, but now it's done?" he asked three times in his unhappy voice.

"Yes, that was fun, but now it's done," we had to say over and over. We finally got him out of the computer store and into the mall, but he was so mad about leaving the computers that he threw himself to the ground and started screaming. I noticed my face felt hot, my palms felt sweaty, and my heart started beating really fast. I wished I could just vanish. I think my Mom did, too. Everyone in the mall was staring at us. Mom handed me the shopping bag to hold so she could use both of her hands. She kneeled next to him and tried to get him up. He just wouldn't budge. Finally, she started making up a song, and she sang it to him. The song was to the tune of "Mary Had a Little Lamb" and it went like this:

> *Let's get up and walk to the car,*
>
> *Walk to the car, walk to the car.*
>
> *When you are all buckled in your seat,*
>
> *You can look at pictures on my phone.*

He calmed down immediately. He loves when Mom sings to him. I guess he liked that her song included a line about looking at pictures on her phone. So he got up and started walking. That's when I noticed some teenagers, pointing and staring at us. I really wanted to disappear.

<u>What Mikey Loves</u>

Computers

Routines

Looking at pictures on
Mom's phone

The number 22

Saying the same thing 3
times in a row

Being TNW
(The Neighborhood Watch)

Chapter Seven

Dad Saves the Day

When we first got home from the mall, Michael went to his room to be the Neighborhood Watch. Looking out his window always seems to calm him down. I heard Mom on the phone with Dad. Her voice was quiet, but I could hear that she used the words "exhausted" and "impossible" on her end of the conversation. I guess she was telling Dad about our mall experience.

About twenty minutes later, Dad walked through the door. He was home from work earlier than usual, but sometimes he does that on Fridays.

When he saw my shopping bag from Polka Dots, I could tell he was about to ask me, "So, how was the mall?" But then he closed his mouth and just gave me a hug. I guess he realized, after his phone conversation with Mom, that asking me about our time at the mall wouldn't be a great question.

Dad announced, "Katie, you and Mom are going to have a girls' night tonight. You get to choose a restaurant and go back to the mall if you would like." Then he added, "Mikey and I are going to have a boys' night."

Sometimes, Dad can save the day just like that. He knew Mom and I both needed a break from Michael, and I think both of my parents realized that Michael and the mall just do not mix well.

It turned out to be a fun night. Usually, Mom is focused on making sure I eat the right stuff at each meal. But tonight, we relaxed and just had our favorite guacamole and chips for dinner at a Mexican restaurant near the mall. Then we went to a few more stores. I found two pairs of shorts, some short-sleeve tops to match them, and even a pair of new shoes for the spring.

Mom and I decided to treat ourselves to ice cream, and we ate it on our walk out of the mall to the car. "Mom, am I your favorite?" I asked.

"Katie, when you are a mom, you love all of your children the same." That's what she always says.

"But Mom, you know I am the *good* child, right?" I replied.

"You and Mikey are very different from each other, but you are both good," Mom said.

I just don't get it. How can she say Michael and I are both good? He is impossible and exhausting for us to be around. She said so herself on the phone earlier to Dad.

We drove home, and I was smiling on the inside. Eating my ice cream and feeling thankful for my alone time with Mom.

Today I am grateful for

Ice Cream

New Spring Clothes

Time alone with Mom

Chapter Eight

What Is Wrong with Him?

At school, all the teachers know Michael. I wonder if they know me. He always says, "Hello" to everyone in the hallways, even if he doesn't know them. He will go right up to anyone and ask his collection of questions:

What's your name?

How old are you?

When is your garbage day?

Where do you live?

What did you have for breakfast?

41

What are you having for dinner?

He loves routines and schedules. When someone sneezes, he automatically says, "God bless you." If the person doesn't say, "Thank you" immediately, he keeps saying "God bless you" over and over because that is the routine. He is waiting for the "Thank you." Mom says this is all a part of his autism.

Mom says we are lucky that Michael talks at all because some kids with autism don't learn to talk. Sometimes I think we are *not* so lucky because all he does is talk all day asking his strange and embarrassing questions.

I take the bus to school, but Michael takes the van. The van is for kids who have special needs. Some days I wish he could ride the bus with me because I know he would love it. But usually, I'm glad to have a break from him on the way to school. The van picks him up at our driveway and Mom buckles him into his seatbelt. When he gets to school, one of the special education teachers gets him off the van and walks him to his classroom. Kids like me who take the bus don't need a bus seatbelt or a teacher to take us to our classrooms. We just get off the bus and walk by ourselves to our classrooms. I don't know if Michael will ever be able to do that.

Monday morning, as I was walking from the bus to my classroom with my friend, Ally, I heard a familiar noise. It was sort of a cry and partly a scream. Michael was on the ground, having a meltdown because his favorite teacher who gets him off the van was absent and a different teacher had to walk him to his classroom. This is what I mean about routines. If his routine is off at all, he usually has a meltdown. It's annoying enough at home, but to see it at school is the worst.

Ally asked, "Isn't that your brother?" as we walked past him screaming.

"Yes," I quietly replied, wishing I could hug him to make him feel better but also wishing he would just stop screaming. I hate when I feel that way—like I love him and hate him at the same time.

"What is wrong with him?" Ally asked. "Is he

OK?"

There it was again: the rude, dreaded question. Why do people always ask me what is wrong with him?

"Sure, he'll be fine," I muttered. She wouldn't get it anyway. Her brother doesn't have autism.

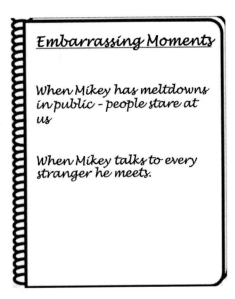

Embarrassing Moments

When Mikey has meltdowns in public - people stare at us

When Mikey talks to every stranger he meets.

Chapter Nine

The Playdate Disaster

I couldn't wait for school to end on Monday. I was looking forward to my first playdate with my friend, Mia that afternoon. When I have playdates at our house, Mom usually buys a delicious snack, like cookies or brownies from the bakery. I could taste them already!

Mia and I stepped off the bus and ran in through the front door. As expected, Mom had some chocolate bakery cookies along with some sliced apples waiting for us as our after-school snack. She always tries to balance out the cookies with some fruit. I eat the fruit just to get more cookies!

"Hi, girls. How was third grade today?" Mom asked. That was her usual after-school question.

I replied with my standard, "Good," but Mia went on and on about the science lesson and the assembly we had that afternoon and even told Mom about our lesson with Mrs. Peters from Friday. Mom looked interested and kept asking questions until I gave her a look that meant to leave us alone.

I heard some thudding on the stairs as Michael came down from his room to see us. I could feel my stomach tighten, as I prepared for whatever embarrassing moment would come next.

"Hi, Katie! Hi, Katie! Hi, Katie!" he said way too loudly.

"Hi, Mikey," I replied, without as much enthusiasm.

"Is this Ally?" he asked, grabbing her arm. He is always mixing up the names of my friends.

"No, Mikey, this is Mia," I told him as I noticed

Mia pulling her arm away from his grasp.

"Hi, Mikey," Mia said in a high-pitched voice that I imagined she would use when talking to a three-year-old. "I know you from school. I see you when you deliver Mrs. Magee's mail to our classroom."

"OK," Michael said.

Sometimes he doesn't know what to say, so he just says "OK." Then he turned around and went up to his room. I told myself to relax.

With Michael up in his room playing on his tablet, we had the kitchen to ourselves. Well, Mom was there too, putting away some groceries.

As we were sitting, chatting and enjoying our cookies, I noticed that Mia had stopped talking all of a sudden. There was a strange look on her face. She was looking toward the stairs. I think Mom noticed the sudden silence, too and looked over at us. Michael was shrieking with delight upstairs—a sound Mom and I are so used to hearing, we barely notice it anymore.

"What is that noise?" Mia asked with an uncomfortable look on her face.

"What noise?" I replied.

"I hear something coming from upstairs," Mia said.

"Oh, that's just Mikey."

"What is he *doing*? Is he laughing or crying?" Mia sounded a little concerned.

Mom interrupted, "He's excited because he just got an e-mail on his tablet from someone. Probably from Mrs. Oh or Mrs. Strickland, his favorite teachers."

"Oh, he knows how to e-mail? That's cool." Mia continued, "Does he always make those noises? Your house is loud!"

Mom and I paused. Mia is the oldest of three kids, and I'll bet her house is loud too. I've seen her brother and sister at the playground, and they make a lot of noise. But deep down, I knew what she meant, and it hurt my feelings. Michael's happy sounds are so different from most other kids' sounds of happiness.

"Yes, all houses with kids are loud sometimes," Mom said quietly. I wondered if Mia's comments made her feel the same way I was feeling.

I heard some banging sounds upstairs. Followed by some foot stomping. Those were the sounds of a meltdown beginning. If Mia thought it was loud when Michael was happy, I could only imagine what she would think about the upcoming meltdown noises.

Luckily, it was sunny and warm out. "Mia, do you want to play outside?" I quickly asked. This way, we could avoid witnessing the meltdown that was in its beginning stages. I wonder what set him off this time?

"Sure, let's go," she said. I think she was just as happy to get away from the noises as I was.

Once we got outside to the swings in our backyard, Mia asked, "So, what is wrong with your brother, anyway?" Again! There it was, the rude question. I have a long list of what is wrong with him, but I wasn't about to share that with Mia.

I really wasn't sure what to say, but here is what came out of my mouth. "He is sort of like the new boy, Adam, joining our class. He has autism." I felt good about my answer. Short, to the point, and true.

"But Michael can talk and Mrs. Peters said that Adam doesn't use words. What did she say again? Non-wordal? And why does your brother make those weird noises?" she continued.

"It's nonverbal, not non-wordal. All kids with autism have things that they are good at and things that are hard for them. Just like anyone else." I realized that I sounded a lot like Mom explaining things to me. I decided not to even try explaining what apraxia is. That's Michael's speech disorder, and it makes him sound different when he talks. His words don't come out clearly, and he forgets how to say words sometimes. He's been going to speech therapy since he was a baby to help him learn to talk.

I couldn't wait for this playdate to be over. I could tell Mia wouldn't want to come back to our house again, and I knew for sure she wasn't going to invite me over to her house. Michael was *seriously* ruining my life.

That night, as Mom was tucking me in, she commented, "So, Mia seems like a nice friend. Did you girls have fun together?"

I was quiet for a moment, trying to settle into my bed, facing the wall instead of looking at Mom. I was trying to think of what to say. I mean, we did have some fun, but I got the feeling that Mia thinks Michael is weird, and that just makes me feel so uncomfortable.

"Yeah, it was okay for a first playdate." I paused. "It was hard because she kept making me feel like I had to explain why Mikey is the way he is. Mom, some kids just don't get it."

"I know what you mean, Katie. Some adults don't get it either," Mom said. "That used to make me feel angry, but then I realized. I can't expect people to understand autism if they don't live with it."

"Mom, do you ever wish Mikey's autism would go away?" I asked.

"Yes, Katie. I used to hope for that all the time. But then I realized that his autism is what makes Mikey the happy, loving, joyful boy he is. Sure, we have to live with his meltdowns. But, think about him." She paused. "He almost always smiles. He compliments us by saying kind things. He never gives up on himself or on us. And he brings a smile to just about everyone he meets. I don't know many other eleven-year-old boys who have those qualities, do you?"

Good point, I thought.

"Katie, I am so lucky I get to be your mom. I know it's not easy for you to be Mikey's sister," she said. "You have to be so patient and wait a long time for attention from Dad and me. I am so proud of you for being so independent and so kind to others."

"Mom, can I tell you something?" I asked.

Her soft smile and nod told me "yes."

"Sometimes wish I had a sister so it wouldn't be just Mikey and me." There, I said it.

As she opened her mouth to reply, I was sure she was going to continue telling me how great it is for me to have Michael in my life, but she surprised me by saying, "Me too, Katie. I know you must get lonely, not having anyone around the house to play with. It's hard to only play Mikey's games."

I'm lucky—Mom gets it.

I am NEVER EVER inviting a friend over again

Mikey is ruining my life

He makes strange noises

He is so loud and annoying

He always embarrasses me

I hate watching people talk to him like he is a baby

Chapter Ten

Adam's First Day

The next day was Adam's first day in our class. When I arrived in the classroom, he was already at his seat with Mrs. Strickland, his teacher's aide. I was so happy to see that she was his aide. Mrs. Strickland was one of Michael's favorites from when he was in first grade. If she could handle Michael's meltdowns, then she could handle anything!

When Bella arrived, she walked straight over to Adam's desk without using her walker and said, "Welcome to our class, Adam!" She had made a welcome card with some drawings for him, and she put it on his desk. Bella always thinks of kind things to do for others. I wished I had thought to make him a card, too. Adam looked at Bella for a moment, and I think he almost smiled at her.

Mia walked over to Adam's desk and said, "Hi, Adam," in that same, babyish voice she used with Michael at our playdate. I can't stand it when kids my age talk to kids who have special needs like they're babies. I wish they would just talk to him in a regular voice, like they talk to anyone else our age.

Mrs. Magee started the day as usual with attendance and lunch count. After the Pledge of Allegiance, we had a writing assignment. I noticed Adam was making a grunting noise. Out of the corner of my eye, I saw something flying in the air, and I realized it was Adam's pencil which he had just thrown to the floor. Mrs. Strickland handed Adam a small Rubik's cube that was not solved. Adam stopped grunting instantly and started working on the Rubik's cube. He had it solved in about a minute. I couldn't believe it! I'd never seen anyone solve a

Rubik's cube so quickly!

Next was Spanish class. That can get loud because we have to do some singing in Spanish. I noticed Adam was wearing really cool-looking green headphones, but they weren't plugged into anything. After Spanish, I asked Mrs. Strickland about the headphones and she let me try on a pair. They were awesome! I could still hear what was going on in the classroom, but they made everything quieter so I could concentrate better. It was sort of like being underwater. All of the classroom sounds were dulled. I guess those headphones helped Adam, too.

I didn't see Adam during lunch or recess, but when we got back from recess, he was at his desk. He looked ready for our math lesson, with a pencil in his hand. I noticed two solved Rubik's cubes in Mrs. Strickland's small "bag of tricks" (that is what she calls her bag with lots of helpful but quiet toys in it). Mrs. Magee has been working with us on long division, and it is really hard. She is a great math teacher, but I still have trouble with long division. During math, she calls on students to show their work on the whiteboard and then explain how they got their answers. I hardly ever raise my hand during math because I don't want to get something wrong, especially if I'm writing it on the board.

I saw Adam raising his hand a lot during math. When Mrs. Magee called on him, he ran right up to the board and got the math problem right! He jumped up and down and flapped his arms a little bit when he was done. His handwriting wasn't neat, but I could read the numbers.

I saw Timmy look at Olivia with a smirk on his face. When Mrs. Magee turned her back to write the next problem on the board, they flapped their hands under their desks and silently laughed together. I knew what they were up to and couldn't believe how rude they were.

I heard Mrs. Strickland whisper into Adam's ear what sounded like a little song, telling him he did a good job. It made me think of Mom, using songs with Michael to keep him calm.

I wrote on a sticky note "You are good at

math," and stuck it on Adam's desk when the math lesson was over. Mrs. Strickland smiled at me, and Adam flapped when he read my note. It felt good inside to know that I made Adam smile with his whole body.

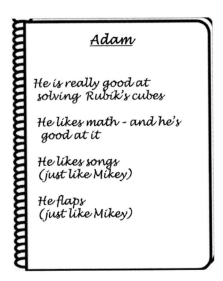

Chapter Eleven

Getting It

After school, I had dance class, and when Ally's mom dropped me off at home in the late afternoon, I noticed the house was quieter than usual. Mom was at her desk working, and Michael was nowhere to be seen. I knew he was home, but it was strange that I could not see or hear him. He usually waits by the door for me and asks whoever dropped me off to beep their horn as they pull out of the driveway. Then he asks me all about dance class. He wants to know who was there and who was absent.

That's his routine. I guess I sort of missed *not* having him at the door.

"Hi Mom, where's Mikey?" I asked.

"He's in his room, being the Neighborhood Watch." Mom continued, "That big truck we saw last week is our new neighbor moving in, so he's been watching the moving men carry in their furniture and boxes very quietly from his room." She smiled calmly. "How was dance?"

"It was good. We're learning a new dance routine for our recital. Want me to show you?" I asked eagerly.

"Sure, now is a great time to show me your dance," Mom said.

I love when Mom doesn't have to focus on Michael and can give me her full attention without chasing him or watching his every move. Right now, she was watching my dance moves, and it felt great to make her smile.

"Wow! Katie, that is a beautiful dance!" Mom said when I was finished.

"Mom, we have a new student in our class, and he is sort of like Mikey," I told her.

"Oh, really? How is he like Mikey?" she asked.

"Well, he flaps, and I think he has autism. He's nonverbal, and he has Mrs. Strickland with him all the time," I said. "Some kids make fun of him. Do you think the kids in Mikey's class make fun of him?" I asked.

"I think there will always be people in this world who just don't get it," she said. "It's our job, as people who *do* get it, to be leaders and role models to those who don't."

"What do you mean?" I asked.

Mom thought about it. "We can show them how to accept people for who they are and to appreciate the differences. Like when you were a helper at the Unified Sports program. You were there as a partner to a student who has a disability, right?"

"Yes, I was Bella's partner," I said.

"Well, do you accept Bella for who she is even though she is so different from you?"

"Yes, Bella is awesome!" I said.

"What makes her so awesome?" Mom asked.

I thought for a moment, and then I started to list Bella's awesome qualities. "She is kind to everyone. She always smiles. She goes out of her way to say nice things to people. She is fun to be around."

"Well, Katie, you are already on your way. You are helping the people who don't get it by being yourself," she said. "Bella's mom told me that some kids don't want to be her friend because she is a little bit different. You like being her friend because you found all the great qualities that you enjoy about Bella. You look beyond her differences and you like her for the person she is."

I'd never thought of it that way before. Me, a role model, to help others get it.

Bella

She is kind

She makes people smile

*Walking is hard for her,
but she never complains*

*She is really good at
horseback riding*

*She is a great listener
and friend*

Chapter Twelve

New Neighbors

"Katie, let's walk down to the new neighbor's house and welcome them to the neighborhood with this plate of cookies," Mom said.

"Why? No one ever welcomed us when we moved in with a plate of cookies," I asked. I really didn't want to go with her to meet the new neighbors. It was probably a family with older kids, just like everyone else on our street.

"Because it's a kind thing to do," Mom replied.

I knew she was right. I would have loved a

plate of cookies when we first moved in. "OK, I'll go get my shoes."

"I'll go help Mikey get ready to go," she said.

"Does he *have* to come?" I asked, as I imagined all the embarrassing questions he would ask our new neighbors. I wanted to make a good first impression and that did not include bringing Michael with us.

"Katie, I can't leave him here alone. Besides, getting out will be good for him." She was always saying things like that.

Mom went into the family room where Michael was looking out the window. I heard her say, "Mikey, please look at me," and then she started singing (to the tune of "Mary Had a Little Lamb" of course):

> *Mikey–in two minutes from now,*
> *we will put on our shoes,*
> *then we will walk down*
> *to meet our new neighbors.*
> *We will say hello and introduce ourselves,*
> *We will give them some cookies,*
> *Then we will say good-bye and come home*

She doesn't have the best singing voice, but Michael really listens to her when she sings the directions. "Again! Again! Again!" he begged. So she had to sing it two more times, and by the end, he was singing along with her.

We started walking to the house, and I noticed a purple bike, about my size, in the new neighbor's driveway. *Could it be that a girl my age moved in?* I didn't want to get my hopes up, but I know it would be awesome to have a new friend who lived so close.

My heart was beating fast as my mom urged me to ring the doorbell. A woman came to the door, and immediately Michael asked, "What's your name? How old are you?" The woman had a warm smile.

Mom quickly said, "Mikey, remember, we don't ask adults their ages." She followed up with, "Hi, I'm Anna, and these are my children, Michael and Katie. We wanted to welcome your family to the neighborhood. We live just two doors down." She extended her arms to hand the plate of cookies to our smiling new neighbor.

"Oh, thank you so much!" our new neighbor said. "I'm Stephanie. It's nice to meet you all. My daughter, Lauren, will love these!" She paused and then said, "Katie, is that your name?"

I quickly nodded yes.

"How old are you?" she asked.

"Nine," I answered shyly.

"I thought so! Lauren just turned ten last month. She was hoping to have a new friend on our street! She's out with her dad right now buying some flowers to plant in the front yard, but when they get home, I'll have her stop by. Is your house the blue one?"

"Yes. Maybe we can go for a bike ride. I'll show her around," I said.

"She will love that! I'll send her down with her bike to ring your doorbell when she gets home," Stephanie said.

Then, from inside the house, I heard an odd sound. It sounded like a man was crying. My face must have looked concerned, or maybe confused, because Stephanie said, "Oh, that's just Jimmy. He's watching his favorite show. He laughs really loud. Do you want to come in and meet him?"

"Sure," my Mom and I said together. I think we were both curious to see the inside of the house and to meet the person who made such odd noises. Michael was already in the garage, wheeling around their garbage and recycling cans. "Garbage cans are his 'thing,'" my mom told Stephanie. She smiled and nodded, as if she understood exactly what Mom meant. *"Come on inside, Mikey,"* Mom sang. He actually listened and came inside. I think he just wanted to see where all the light switches were in the house so he could turn the lights on and off. Yes, that is another of my brother's favorite things to do. Turn lights on and off.

We walked into the house and I noticed there were boxes everywhere. I could tell that Stephanie was busy unpacking when we rang her doorbell a few minutes ago. There was a boy—actually he looked more like a man—sitting in a wheelchair and watching *Sesame Street* on TV. I guessed this was Jimmy. Michael went right up to him and asked, "What's your name? How old are you?"

"This is my son, Jimmy. He is fifteen. Jimmy is Lauren's big brother," Stephanie told us.

I heard a yelping noise come from Jimmy, and then a grunt. His body was shaking as he pointed toward the TV. Next, he made that odd noise I heard from outside that I thought was a man crying. I quickly realized it was the way Jimmy laughed!

"Jimmy doesn't talk with words. He uses his body and some noises to communicate. You'll get used to it soon," Stephanie told us.

I was trying to act like I wasn't surprised at Jimmy's loud sounds. I was also trying to act like I wasn't bewildered that he was fifteen years old and watching *Sesame Street*. But I think my mouth was hanging open in disbelief.

"Hi, Jimmy. I'm Anna and this is Katie," I heard Mom say. "I think you already met Mikey."

"UhhUhhUhh," said Jimmy. And I think he

was trying to smile at us.

"Jimmy, our new neighbors brought us cookies!" Stephanie said. I heard more loud noises from Jimmy. "Jimmy, you love cookies." Then, Stephanie turned to face Mom and me. She said, "I know he's loud, but I promise, you will get used to him." She was still smiling.

I just wanted to get out of there. "Mom, can we go now?" I whispered into her ear.

Mom ignored me and said, "We're so glad to have new neighbors. You'll like our street. It's quiet and safe, and lots of very nice families live here. If you have any questions, you know, about where to go for haircuts, or the name of a dentist, or good places for pizza, just let me know. I also have some great babysitters."

"Thank you so much." Stephanie smiled. "We are so glad to be here. We moved to this town for the schools. Our old town didn't have great special education services for Jimmy, and we've heard terrific reports about the special education programs here."

"Well, I'm somewhat of an expert in special education too." Mom smiled as she motioned her head toward Michael. "So I can also help you out with any of those questions."

"I think I'm going to like it here," replied Stephanie.

I tugged on Mom's sleeve again, trying to get her to leave. But she and Stephanie continued their conversation. Soon I zoned out into my own world. All I could hear was Jimmy making his noises, and all I could see was the lights being flicked on and then off again by Michael. I couldn't wait to leave.

My Neighborhood

Good for bike riding

I wish there were more kids my age to play with

Too many teenagers

Great climbing trees

Chapter Thirteen

Hanging Out

When we got home, I was mad at myself. I was upset that I felt so uncomfortable around Jimmy. I'm supposed to "get it," and I sure didn't act that way when I met Jimmy. I acted the way Mia acted at our playdate a few days ago.

I didn't have time to think about it for long because the next thing I knew, the doorbell rang. It was Lauren, our new neighbor.

"Hi, I'm Lauren. My mom said I just missed meeting you at our new house." Wow, she was so friendly and not shy at all.

"Hi, Lauren, I'm Katie," I replied. I tried my best to match her enthusiasm with a friendly smile.

I heard Michael's thumping footsteps behind me in the hallway. He was coming to see who was at the door. He began with his favorite questions. "What's your name? How old are you?"

"Are you Mikey? My mom told me that you might ask me those questions. I'm Lauren, and I am ten years old," she easily replied, giving Michael the same smile she gave to me. I noticed right away how comfortable she was around him and that she talked to him like he was a typical eleven-year-old rather than a boy with autism. I liked her a lot already.

After introducing Lauren to Mom, I asked her if she wanted to play inside or outside. We decided to hang out in my room. She asked me about school, and I told her all about the lockers, air conditioning and teachers. She was in fourth grade so we wouldn't be in the same class, but we would be on the same bus!

We were sitting on my beanbag chair, and I was showing her some photos of my friends and family. Even though we'd just met, she felt like someone I'd known for a long time. I guess we just clicked.

"You're lucky he can talk," I heard Lauren say as she looked at a picture in my photo album of Michael and me together.

"What?" I asked.

"You're lucky that Michael can talk to you. My brother, Jimmy, has cerebral palsy, and he will never be able to talk. I always wish that he could talk to me."

I didn't know what to say. Lauren continued, "I try to think about all the things Jimmy *can* do. He can laugh. He can smile. He can look at me, and it feels like he is talking to me with his eyes sometimes. He can love. He can eat pizza. Oh boy, can he ever eat pizza! Once he ate an entire pizza. That's all eight slices of a large pizza!"

We both started laughing. She went on about the things that Jimmy *can* do. It was cool listening to her talk about her brother.

"Have you ever been to Sibshops?" she asked.

"What's that?" I replied.

"They had it in my old town. It's a group for kids like us. You know, kids who have siblings with disabilities. By the way, what does Michael have? Is it autism?"

"Yes," I responded. But I didn't feel embarrassed like I did when Mia was here for the playdate. I felt completely comfortable with Lauren. She totally gets it.

"Anyway," she went on, "we did lots of fun things at Sibshops. The teacher who ran it was great. I thought it was going to be a boring class where we had to sit around and talk about our lives with our siblings who have different disabilities. But that was not it at all. We got to play games, go on field trips, and every once in a while we shared about how our lives are different from our other friends' lives. The Sibshops group I used to go to isn't that far away. Do you want to go with me next time I go?"

I was so glad she invited me. "Definitely!"

What I'm Looking Forward To

Going to Sibshops with
 Lauren someday

Having a new neighbor who
 is (almost) my age!

Chapter Fourteen

The Bike Ride Chat

The next day was Lauren's first day at school. Of course, we sat together on the bus, and I showed her how to get to the main office so Mrs. Peters could show her how to find her new classroom. That's another part of Mrs. Peters's job. Helping new students feel comfortable in school.

Since I am in third grade and Lauren is in fourth grade, we had the same recess period. I easily found her as soon as recess started. We decided to play hopscotch on the blacktop first, and then we played on the monkey bars together. It felt like I'd known her for a lot longer than one day. Out of the corner of my eye, I saw some of the soccer kids (that's what I call the kids who always play soccer at recess) making strange jumping movements on the field. It didn't look like soccer moves to me. Once I started really watching them, I knew immediately what they were doing. They were copying Adam. Their arms were flapping, and they were all laughing. I tried to ignore it, but I couldn't. I pointed it out to Lauren. I could tell she knew right away what was going on out there, too. She had a look on her face, like she was getting a good idea.

The recess teacher blew the whistle, signaling the end of recess. Lauren and I said goodbye to each other as she headed to the fourth grade line and I dashed over to the third grade line. I was looking forward to sitting with her on the bus ride home that afternoon.

Later, on the bus, Lauren said her first day was pretty good. She was exhausted, but she still wanted to go on a bike ride with me around the neighborhood. We spent so much time hanging out in my room yesterday that we ran out of time for our bike ride. So today was my neighborhood cycling tour for Lauren. We decided to each go home to drop our backpacks off and grab a quick snack. Then we would meet up for the bike ride. As I waited for Lauren at the end of my driveway, our designated meeting spot, I could hear Michael behind me in the garage. He was reaching for his bike—it still has training wheels. "Katie! Katie! Katie! I want to ride my bike with you," he shouted out to me.

"Mikey, there is someone on the phone for you!" I heard Mom call from the garage door. Sometimes she calls my grandma or my aunt to talk to Michael on the phone when he needs a distraction. *Good timing, Mom. Thanks*! I looked down toward Lauren's driveway and saw she was on her way over to meet me. Michael loves phone calls. He forgot all about wanting to tag along on my bike ride. He dropped his bike and ran inside to take the phone call.

As Lauren and I rode around, I pointed out the

houses that always have the best Halloween candy. I showed her the dirt path that leads to the playground. I love the feeling of having control over my bike, gliding so fast down the hills. With the wind in my hair and the sun on my face, I was feeling so free. I had that awesome feeling in my heart. The one I get when I make a new friend. But this time, the feeling was even bigger because this friend really gets it about Michael.

We stopped our bikes at the end of the street and put down our kickstands. I showed Lauren the gigantic climbing tree. We climbed up the tree and sat down on the big branch together, letting our feet swing in the air. We had to catch our breath before heading back to our houses for homework and dinner.

"Lauren?" I asked, "do people ever ask you questions about Jimmy?"

"Sometimes people ask questions like, 'Was he born like that?' or 'Is he contagious?' Sometimes people just stare. I don't know which is worse. The staring or the rude questions," she replied.

"People always ask me, 'What is wrong with your brother?' I think I'll scream if I have to hear that one more time," I confided in my new friend.

"I totally know what you mean," she replied. "I wish I could just tell the people who stare at him, 'He's a person, and he has feelings, too!'" Lauren continued, "I think when people look at him, they just think to themselves *He's in a wheelchair and he can't even talk.* Meanwhile, they don't know anything about him and all the things he *can* do."

"I never thought of it that way," I admitted. "To think of all the things Mikey *can* do."

Lauren gets it. I get it. But most people at school don't get it. Even our teachers don't really get it. How can I expect them to understand? They don't live with a brother who has a disability.

Lauren had that look on her face again, like she had a good idea. "I think there's something we can do about this. To make people stop staring and asking the rude questions," she said.

"Really? What can we do?" I was curious.

Just then, I heard Michael's voice shouting, "Katie! Katie! Katie! Dinner! Dinner! Dinner!" He really does love saying things three times. Lauren smiled at me. I remembered what she said about wishing Jimmy could talk.

"Well, I guess I have to go now. I'll see you on the bus tomorrow?" I said.

"Definitely!" Lauren smiled.

That night, after dinner, I was alone in my room, sitting at my desk. I was supposed to be doing my homework, but it was too hard to concentrate. All I could think about was my conversation with Lauren on the tree branch about Michael and Jimmy. I couldn't wait to hear what her idea was.

How I feel like the Big Sister (even though I am the Little Sister)

My bike = 2 wheeler
Mikey's bike = training wheels

Me = bus to school
Mikey = van to school

Me = sleepovers with friends
Mikey = no sleepovers

Me = watch shows for kids my age
Mickey = watches baby shows

Me = showers
Mikey = baths

Chapter Fifteen

Recess

The next day at recess, I introduced Lauren to some of my friends, and we ended up playing jump rope with a big group of third and fourth grade girls. As I was turning the jump rope for my friends to jump, I noticed the soccer kids flapping and jumping on the field just like they were doing the day before. My first instinct was to find one of the recess teachers and show her what was going on. I said to Lauren, "Come on, let's go tell on those kids. They aren't being nice."

"They just don't get it yet," Lauren replied.

"But they are being so mean out there," I said. "I wish they would just stop."

Lauren had that familiar look on her face, and I could tell she was deep in thought. "Let's ask Mrs. Peters if we can help her."

"Help Mrs. Peters? With what?" I asked, but I don't think Lauren heard me. She was already walking away from recess and toward the school.

We asked the recess teacher if we could go inside the school to talk to Mrs. Peters. She was sitting at her desk eating lunch when we knocked on her door. "Hello girls, come on in!" Mrs. Peters smiled as we entered her office. She saw the determined looks on our faces and asked, "What's up? You two look like you have something important on your minds."

"Mrs. Peters," Lauren began, "Katie and I were wondering if we can help you with something?"

"I love helpers. Help me with what?" she asked.

"Well, Katie and I notice that lots of kids at this school just don't understand about disabilities. Even though they're in the same classes with kids who have special needs and disabilities, they still make fun and ask rude questions," Lauren said.

"Well, I do teach lessons to help students understand about disabilities and learning differences. But maybe I need your help. After all, you girls are the true experts. Can you think of a way we can help your classmates understand special needs and disabilities better?" she asked.

Our eyes got big and our imaginations even bigger! "Yes!" We both nodded our heads.

Recess
(the good stuff)

Jump rope

Monkey bars

Hanging out with my friends

Recess
(the not-so-good stuff)

When kids are mean

When it's freezing cold

Chapter Sixteen

Making Lists

Lauren and I got right to work. I went to her house after school. We went up to her room and started by making a list of all the rude questions that people have ever asked us about our own brothers. As always, I had my notebook full of lists with me in my backpack. We both loved making lists, so it was easy for us to get our ideas down onto paper. Here is what we came up with:

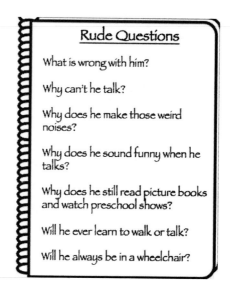

Rude Questions

What is wrong with him?

Why can't he talk?

Why does he make those weird noises?

Why does he sound funny when he talks?

Why does he still read picture books and watch preschool shows?

Will he ever learn to walk or talk?

Will he always be in a wheelchair?

Next, we decided to make a second list. This list included what we wished kids our age could understand about disabilities.

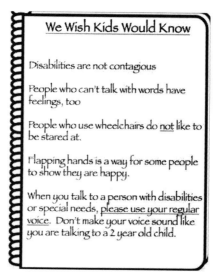

We Wish Kids Would Know

Disabilities are not contagious

People who can't talk with words have feelings, too

People who use wheelchairs do not like to be stared at.

Flapping hands is a way for some people to show they are happy.

When you talk to a person with disabilities or special needs, please use your regular voice. Don't make your voice sound like you are talking to a 2 year old child.

We read over our lists and we knew we were off to a great start. We were both good at making lists!

"So, what's next?" I asked Lauren.

"Well, I was thinking. We can turn our lists into a presentation on the computer," Lauren said.

Presentation? Isn't that when you speak to a group of people? My heart raced, and my stomach did a nervous flip. Did Lauren really think that I would be able to stand up in front of the class at school and teach the other kids about this? I forgot that she'd only known me for a short time and didn't really know how shy and worried I usually am. I guess I haven't been quite so shy or worried since meeting Lauren. I paused and then asked, "Are you thinking that we're going to be the ones to get up in front of the classes and make a presentation from our lists?"

Lauren smiled. "Bingo! Great idea, Katie!"

My heart sank. *How was I going to tell her that I didn't know if I had the courage to do that?*

"I thought we were just going to make the lists

and give them to Mrs. Peters. But your idea that *we* are the ones to get up and give the presentation *with* Mrs. Peters is brilliant!" Lauren said excitedly.

I took a deep breath. "Lauren, I don't know if I can do that."

"What do you mean? Of course you can." Lauren's voice sounded encouraging.

"I've never done anything like this before," I said.

"Katie, we will be together. Plus, you heard what Mrs. Peters said. *We* are the true experts. We *have* to do this!" Lauren encouraged me.

I got caught up in her enthusiasm and said, "OK, let's do this!"

"Lauren! Katie!" We heard Lauren's mom, Stephanie, call up the stairs to us. "Do you girls want a snack?"

"Yes. We'll be right down, Mom," Lauren said.

When we got downstairs, Stephanie had strawberries in a bowl and a plateful of chocolate-chip cookies. Yum!

"Thanks, Mom," Lauren said. Then she turned to me. "Let's eat in the TV room so Jimmy won't be alone."

"OK," I said as I followed Lauren, holding the snacks while she carried our water glasses.

"Hi, Jimmy. Can we watch Elmo with you?" Lauren asked as she set down the water and gave Jimmy a hug.

"UMM-UMM!" Jimmy exclaimed. I could tell he was happy we were with him. Lauren's mom was right. I was already used to his noises. Michael's noises were different from Jimmy's, but I guess I'm used to living in a loud house!

Lauren started singing along to the songs on *Sesame Street* for Jimmy and he laughed. I smiled, knowing that Lauren and I were meant to be neighbors and friends.

Lauren

She is really smart

She has good GREAT ideas

She is fun

We have a LOT in common

She is easy to get along with

Chapter Seventeen

A True Expert

When I got home from Lauren's house, it was almost dinner time, and Mom was cooking. I was bubbly and excited after spending the afternoon with Lauren. Just as I started to tell Mom all about the project that Lauren and I were working on, Michael walked into the kitchen.

"Hi, Katie! Hi, Katie! Hi, Katie!" he said, three times of course.

"Hi, Mikey." I heard music coming out of the

iPod he was holding in his hand. "What song are you listening to?" I asked.

"'The Wheels on the Bus'! My favorite! Sing with me, Katie!" shouted Michael.

I followed him into the family room, and we started singing together. "*The horn on the bus goes beep, beep, beep.*" I'm not usually this interested in singing his preschool songs with him, but something about watching Lauren with Jimmy earlier this afternoon made me want to sing with Michael.

After dinner, while Mom was giving Michael a bath and getting him ready for bed, I told Dad all about how Lauren and I were going to help Mrs. Peters at school.

"We're helping with something very important," I told him. "Mrs. Peters said she needs our help because we are true experts."

"Well, Katie, I know you're smart, but what are you an expert in these days?" he asked.

"Disabilities. Special needs. Living with a brother who has autism," I replied.

"Yes, I have to agree. You are definitely an expert in those areas. What sort of help are you giving to Mrs. Peters?" asked Dad.

"Lauren and I want kids at our school to understand disabilities better. We're making a presentation on the computer."

"Wow, that sounds official! Do you need help getting your ideas into a computer presentation? You know I do a lot of presentations for my work. I guess you could say I'm somewhat of an expert on the computer," Dad said with a smile.

"I think Lauren and I want to do this all on our own, Dad. But if we need help, I'll let you know," I said.

"Good night, Katie. Good night, Katie. Good night, Katie," I heard Michael call from the top of the stairs.

I walked to the bottom of the stairs so I could see Mikey. I put my hands in the air on an imaginary steering wheel, pretending to drive a bus, and then beeped my imaginary horn three times.

Michael laughed and sang along, "*The horn on the bus goes beep, beep, beep.*" He begged, "Katie, again, again, again!"

"OK, Mikey. One more time." I smiled. It felt good to play together, even though it was a preschool song. I loved making him laugh.

Mom came down a few minutes later. I finished telling her about my project with Lauren. She listened and said, "I can't wait to see the presentation, Katie. It sounds awesome and I agree with Mrs. Peters. You and Lauren are true experts."

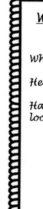

<u>*What makes me smile*</u>

When I make Mikey laugh

Hearing a funny joke

Having something great to look forward to

Chapter Eighteen

The Missing Piece

Our project was moving along quickly. We worked harder on the presentation than we did on our homework assignments! We did end up using Dad's computer skills to get our lists and ideas into the presentation after all. Dad was able to insert pictures and even some music into it. We were almost finished, and we knew it was good, but we felt like it was missing something.

During recess, we visited Mrs. Peters to tell her that we were almost done. I had asked Dad to e-mail the presentation to Mrs. Peters last night so she could take a look. She opened it on her computer and smiled. "This is really awesome, girls. I know you will be very successful with your goal. This presentation will definitely help your classmates understand disabilities better."

"Thank you," Lauren and I said at the same time.

"We feel like it is missing something, but we're not quite sure what it needs," I said.

Lauren nodded in agreement.

Just then, I heard the familiar sound of Bella's happy whistling. She was coming by to visit Mrs. Peters for her weekly meeting. I have a weekly meeting with her too. That is when I can talk to her about my worries. I wonder what Bella talks about with her.

"Hi, Bella!" I said. "Have you met my friend, Lauren?"

"Hi, Katie! Nice to meet you Lauren," Bella replied. "What are you guys doing here? Did you have lunch bunch?"

In that moment, something clicked for me. I knew exactly what was missing from our presentation! I turned to look at Lauren, and she had a huge smile and was nodding her head at me. Good friends think alike!

"We're working on a project about disabilities," Lauren explained.

"Oh, that sounds really cool," Bella said. "What kind of project?"

"We're making a presentation on the computer to teach kids what we wish they would understand about disabilities," I said. "Would you be interested in working on it with us? After all, YOU are a true expert in this area."

"Sure, I'd love to help you guys." Bella smiled.

We showed her some of our presentation on the computer. She really liked the part that showed our lists. Bella reached for some paper and a pencil. She started writing her own list right away.

Mrs. Peters loved the idea of Bella helping us. "I don't know why we didn't think of this great idea before." She told us it was time for us to return to our classrooms and Bella's turn to stay. "Bye, Bella!" I said. "Let me know when your list is ready for the presentation."

"I'll have it for you as soon as I get back to class!" said Bella.

Bella! She was our missing piece.

**Feeling Nervous**

My heart beats really fast

My palms get all sweaty

My face gets red and feels warm

My stomach does flips

Chapter Nineteen

Presentation Day

Mrs. Peters met Lauren and me in the hallway outside my classroom. "So, girls, today is the big day. Are you ready to be the teachers today?" she asked.

"We practiced all weekend," Lauren said.

"I'm really nervous, but I think I'm ready," I managed to say, even with the butterflies in my stomach.

Mrs. Peters put her hands out with her palms facing up. Lauren and I each put one of our hands in Mrs. Peters's open hands. My palms were sweaty with nervousness, but I didn't care. Mrs. Peters gets it about anxiety! She gently squeezed our hands and said, "I am so proud of you both! Good luck in there. You are going to do great!"

We could hear Mrs. Magee's voice through the closed classroom door. She was telling my classmates that Mrs. Peters was on her way up for a class lesson. Mrs. Peters let go of our hands and walked into the room to lead the class in some yoga, as usual.

My heart was racing as I anticipated talking in front of my entire class. I suddenly wished I had never agreed to do this presentation. I was shaking, my palms were sweaty, and my stomach was turning. My worries were taking over.

I think Lauren sensed my anxiety. She said, "We can hear Mrs. Peters through the door. Let's do the warrior pose, too."

I felt a little silly doing yoga in the hallway. *What if someone walked by*? But I did it with Lauren anyway. My legs were in a lunge with my arms up in the air. The warrior pose made me feel strong and ready for our presentation. The yoga worked!

Next, we heard Mrs. Peters introducing the guest speakers for today who were "experts in the field of disabilities." That was our signal to walk into the classroom. We opened the classroom door and walked inside. Some of my classmates smiled at us, while others had confused looks on their faces. Mrs. Magee and Mrs. Peters were both beaming.

The computer was ready and plugged into the projector that Dad had set up for us before school that morning.

Just as we had practiced at home, Lauren started by saying, "Hi, everyone. I'm Lauren, and of course you all know Katie. We planned a lesson for your class today. To start, we need some volunteers."

Before she was even done with her sentence, Timmy, Olivia, and a few others who always raised their hands had their arms waving in the air.

We planned that Lauren would call on Olivia and ask her to go into the hallway with Mrs. Peters. While she was out there, Lauren told the class,

"Olivia is going to return to the class in about a minute looking *very* different from how she usually looks. We're going to ask you to stare at her. Please stare especially at the part of her that looks different. You might feel sort of mean or rude staring, but please do it anyway. This is all part of today's lesson." Lauren continued, "I also need three volunteers to act *really* rude." She chose three students with their hands up. I was happy to see that two of them were soccer kids. "For the three of you, your job is to be extra rude. You will point at her, cover your mouth to whisper to your neighbor about her, and laugh just a little bit." The three volunteers nodded in agreement. "Like I said before, you will probably feel mean and rude, but we are just doing this to teach a lesson."

I went to the door to let Mrs. Peters and Olivia know we were ready for them. Mrs. Peters's job was to get Olivia prepared in the hallway.

Olivia walked in slowly with her eyes looking down, wearing the hideous hat that Lauren and I created. It was an old straw hat that had huge, ugly, fake flowers stapled to it. Her face said it all. She looked really uncomfortable. I bet she was regretting that she had raised her hand for this! We didn't want her to feel uncomfortable for too long, so we only had her stand there for thirty seconds. My classmates did an outstanding job with their staring, pointing, and whispering.

When the timer went off, Olivia took the hat off as quickly as she could and used her hands to fix her hair. She asked, "How long was I up there for? It felt like hours."

When we told her it was only thirty seconds, she couldn't believe it. Then, Lauren asked her to tell the class how she had felt. "I felt so embarrassed, and I was wishing I could just take that ugly hat off the whole time."

Lauren asked, "Why did you want to take it off?"

"I didn't like how everyone was pointing at me and staring. And some people were laughing at me."

That was exactly what we were hoping she would say.

I pushed the clicker for our computer presentation to begin. Our list began to show on the screen. It started with:

> Student Presentation – "Getting It"
>
> **People with disabilities have feelings, too.**

It was my turn to talk. I took a deep breath and imagined doing the warrior pose to calm myself down. "The hat Olivia wore is not a special need or a disability. But the hat made her look really different. Olivia told us how uncomfortable she felt because the rest of the class was pointing and staring." I clicked again so more of the ideas on our list were revealed on screen.

> Student Presentation – "Getting It"
>
> **People with disabilities have feelings, too.**
>
> **Please don't point or stare.**

I asked the whole class, "How did you feel when you were staring or pointing at her?"

Mia raised her hand, so I called on her. "You guys were right. I did feel mean staring. It felt like I was hurting her feelings since she was looking down at the ground and not smiling."

One of the soccer kids, Joey, who had volunteered to whisper and laugh at Olivia said, "Yeah, but it was funny to see Olivia in that ugly hat." Some other kids laughed along with him.

Mrs. Peters chimed in, "Yes, the hat was supposed to make Olivia look different. But did you consider how Olivia was feeling when you were laughing at her?"

Joey paused for a moment. He said, "I wasn't thinking about how she was feeling I was just laughing because the hat was so funny looking."

"Thank you for being so honest with us, Joey," said Mrs. Peters. "I think a lot of kids your age forget to think about what other people are feeling. Now that you *are* thinking about it, how do you think the laughing and pointing made Olivia feel?"

"I guess she didn't feel so good," said Joey.

"I have to agree with you, Joey. Olivia didn't feel good at all with people laughing and pointing at her. Our actions can make people feel bad," explained Mrs. Peters.

"Mrs. Magee is always telling us that kindness counts and to be kind to everyone in class. Right, Mrs. Magee?" said Joey.

Mrs. Magee nodded. "I'm glad you were listening to those lessons, Joey. Can anyone share how they plan to be more kind, especially to people with disabilities?"

"Yes, like it says on the screen, not pointing and staring," said Joey.

Wow, a soccer kid was starting to get it! Our presentation seemed to be working.

The next slide showed a picture of Michael flapping his hands. He wasn't smiling with his face, but he was smiling with his whole body. He was standing next to a garbage truck, one of his favorite things in the world.

> Student Presentation – "Getting It"
>
> **Some people with disabilities or special needs flap their hands when they are happy or excited.**
>
> **You can imagine they are smiling with their whole bodies when you see them flapping.**

The classroom was quiet. My classmates seemed really into it. I asked for our next volunteer. Of course, Timmy raised his hand. I walked over to his desk and gave him the ziplock bag that Lauren and I had filled with six crackers and three pieces of bubble gum. "Timmy, your job is to eat these crackers as fast as you can and then try to chew all three pieces of gum."

"No problem for me!" Timmy said eagerly.

"OK. Once you start eating, I will explain the challenge we have set up for you," I told him.

We all giggled a little as we watched Timmy stuff the crackers into his mouth as quickly as he could. Timmy enjoys the spotlight and is used to winning. He is good at sports and always seems to win races. As he was shoving the third piece of gum into his mouth, I revealed his challenge. "Your task is to read these knock-knock jokes to the class." I handed him an index card with the three knock-knock jokes Lauren and I had written out for him to read.

He looked confident. He reached for the index card and tried to tell the jokes. "Ock – ock," he said.

The class knew what he was trying to say with all the gum and crackers in his mouth, so they replied, "Who's there?"

Timmy continued, "Ahhh-nahhhh."

"Ahhh-nahhh who?" we said together, laughing.

Timmy tried to say the punch line of the joke. We couldn't understand him at all. My classmates were saying, "What did you say?" and "What?" He tried again and again. There was more confusion as my classmates now asked, "What did he say?" That's when he gave up. He reached for the tissue box and spat the wad of gum into a tissue. I handed him a bottle of water.

As he was taking a sip, Lauren asked, "Timmy, what was it like to try to talk, but no one could understand you?"

"That was not fun. I didn't like it at all," Timmy said.

"Well, it's not supposed to be *fun*. It's supposed to explain how it feels to be nonverbal," I said. That was not part of how Lauren and I had practiced the presentation. Those words just quickly came out of my mouth. But I felt good about what I'd said.

Mrs. Peters asked, "Were you frustrated, Timmy? How did you feel when you couldn't tell the jokes?"

"Yes, *very* frustrated that no one could understand me," Timmy admitted.

I pushed the clicker again, and up on the screen our list continued:

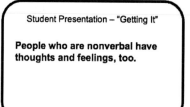

Student Presentation -- "Getting It"

People who are nonverbal have thoughts and feelings, too.

Timmy added, "I didn't like how you guys were saying, 'What did *he* say?' to each other instead of asking me. It made me feel like you didn't even care that I was sitting right there."

Wow, I was impressed that Timmy picked up on that. People are always asking me things like, "How old is he?" when Michael and I are together. I used to answer for him, but now I tell the people who ask, "You can ask him yourself. He can talk." I know he is sometimes hard to understand because of his speech disorder, apraxia, but if you listen really hard and ask him to slow down, it's easier to understand him.

"Everyone, please turn to your writing partner," I said. Mrs. Magee has us paired up with a new writing partner each month for editing and writing, so it was easy to get everyone partnered up.

"Find out which of you is younger." There was some chatter as they talked about birthdays. Mrs. Magee handed me her bell to ring so I could get everyone's attention again. "OK, the younger partner has to pretend to be about two years old. The older partner stays as a third grader."

"What are we supposed to do, change a diaper?" Timmy asked. Everyone laughed. He looked happy that he could talk and joke around again.

"Not quite," I said. "The older partner is going to talk to the younger one the way you would talk to a two-year-old. Ask your partner any of these questions." I clicked and the questions appeared on the screen.

> Student Presentation – "Getting It"
>
> **What's your name?**
>
> **Do you want a cookie?**
>
> **What does a doggie say?**

There was some laughter as my classmates

acted like two-year-olds.

After about a minute, I rang Mrs. Magee's bell to quiet everyone down again. "My first question is for the older partners. What did you notice about the way you talked to your younger partner?"

"I noticed that my voice got higher and I sounded like I was talking to a baby," Bella offered.

"Yes, that's definitely what it sounded like in here," Lauren agreed. "Lots of high voices."

"Here's a question for the younger partners. Did you like it when your partner talked to you in the high-pitched, babyish voice?"

I noticed Mia raising her hand, so I called on her. "I felt like my partner was treating me like I didn't know anything. I didn't like being the two-year-old."

I clicked for our next thought to appear on screen.

Mrs. Peters announced, "Katie and Lauren have another expert who helped them with this presentation. Bella, will you please join the girls in the front of the room?"

Bella already had her smile on her face and her hands on her walker. She was so ready for her part. As she made her way to the front of the classroom, she said, "I know most of you guys have known me since kindergarten. You know me as the girl who has to use a walker. But I would like to tell you some other things about me that you may not know." I pushed the clicker, and Bella's list appeared on the screen.

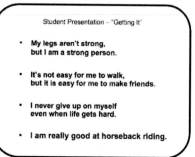

Student Presentation – "Getting It"

- My legs aren't strong,
  but I am a strong person.

- It's not easy for me to walk,
  but it is easy for me to make friends.

- I never give up on myself
  even when life gets hard.

- I am really good at horseback riding.

I looked out at my classmates. All eyes were on Bella as she read her list from the screen. She continued, "It's OK to ask me about my disability, but please ask in a kind way. Please *don't* ask me, 'What's wrong with you?' because there is nothing *wrong* with me. I was just born with legs that are not strong. Instead, you can ask, 'What is it like to *be* you?'"

Bella was a natural teacher. "Olivia, how would it feel if you couldn't take that hat off? Would you rather have people ask you, 'So, what's wrong with your head?' or 'Tell me what it's like to be you.'"

"Um, 'Tell me what it's like to be you' sounds a lot better to me," replied Olivia.

"Exactly," agreed Bella. "For a long time, I had a lot of doctors and nurses focusing on what was wrong with me. I didn't like it. So I decided to only focus on what's right with me."

"Bella, you are really good at horseback riding and making friends." *Wow*, I was impressed to hear this positive comment from Olivia.

"You are really good at drawing and at math, right?" asked Bella.

"Yes," said Olivia.

"It's good to focus on *what's right*," Bella said to the whole class.

"Bella, this gives me a good idea," announced Mrs. Magee. She wrote the words "What's Right with Me?" on the whiteboard to the side of our presentation. "Take out your writer's journals, everyone. Please open your book to the next blank page and write 'What's Right with Me?' at the top of the page. As the day goes on, you can add to your list."

Adam was wearing his headphones throughout the presentation, but he was doodling something with his finger on the classroom tablet. I saw Mrs. Strickland glance at the tablet's screen over his shoulder, and her eyes lit up! She looked over at me with a huge smile.

I wonder what he wrote?

What's Right With Me

I am a good sister

I am great at bike riding, swimming and dancing

I am a kind friend

I am good at baking

I am helpful to others

Chapter Twenty

Adam's Words

The last part of our presentation was very personal because we would be talking about our own brothers.

Lauren went first. I clicked and a picture of Jimmy sitting in his wheelchair appeared on the screen. Lauren said, "Take a look at this picture. You see a young man sitting in a wheelchair. You may be wondering to yourself, *'What's wrong with him? Why is he in a wheelchair?'"*

"No, we are not supposed to ask that,"

interrupted Olivia. "We are supposed to ask, 'Tell me what it's like to be you.' That's what Bella said, and Bella knows!"

Wow again. I was really surprised with how well Olivia was grasping what we were trying to teach the class.

"Yes!" said Mrs. Peters. "Some of you may notice that your mind will sometimes forget to think in this new way. You might think, 'I wonder what's wrong with him? Oops! I mean, I wonder what it's like to be him.'" A few kids nodded their heads.

"I will tell you what it's like to be Jimmy. He has a disability called cerebral palsy. So walking and talking are really hard for him. He has to use a wheelchair to get around." I clicked, and the next photo was of Lauren hugging Jimmy. "Jimmy is my big brother."

I heard a few kids quietly say, "Ohh," as if now they understood why Lauren is an expert.

"Here's what's right with Jimmy," Lauren said. "He enjoys music. He's really good at eating pizza.

He actually speaks to me through his eyes."

"You mean his eyes can talk?" asked Timmy.

"No. He is nonverbal, but I can tell what he is trying to say to me just from looking into his eyes," Lauren explained.

"Wow, cool!" said Timmy.

"Yeah, it's a sibling thing," Lauren said. "He is gentle and kind. He loves it when I sit next to him and read to him. He also likes when I sing songs with him. He really loves when I tell him jokes."

I added, "And he has the best smile."

My thumb pushed the presentation clicker, and the next picture was of Michael. We'd chosen a flapping photo of him for the presentation. I was nervous the kids would laugh at the picture, but they didn't. They just waited for me to start talking.

Bella raised her hand and asked, "So, what's it like to be Michael?"

"Well," I began, "he's a happy kid who loves meeting new people. He has autism, so communication is difficult for him. He can talk, but his words don't always match his feelings. He doesn't always know what to say or how to answer questions. He likes routines so that he can know exactly when things are going to happen. He gets tired quickly. He likes to laugh and have fun. He does not like fire drills or loud noises. He likes to say things three times. He flaps when he is excited. Just like in this picture." I took a deep breath and clicked to the next picture of Michael and me together. "Here's what's right with Michael. He is a great reader. He claps for me every time I shoot a basketball or sing a song with him. He makes people around him smile. He always makes sure everyone has a turn at whatever game is going on. He smiles with his whole body when he is happy and flapping."

Just then, I noticed that Adam was raising his hand. He had the classroom tablet in his hand. I walked over to him and he handed me the tablet. I silently read what he wrote and asked him, "May I read this to the class?" He nodded his head yes. I took another deep breath and began reading Adam's words from the tablet screen to my classmates.

It is hard being me because I want to say words.

But my words won't come out.

I am lucky that I can read and write.

I am good at soccer and math.

I am good at solving Rubik's cubes.

I looked at him, and he looked back at me. I remembered that Adam had a hard time looking at people's eyes, so I knew this meant a lot. We smiled at each other as I handed him back the tablet.

The last idea on our list went up on the screen as we ended our part of the presentation:

Student Presentation – "Getting It"

And remember....

Disabilities are NOT contagious

Best Moments of our Presentation

When Adam used the tablet to tell us all about him

Once we started, I wasn't that nervous after all

Olivia really gets it now

Chapter Twenty-One

We Did It

"We did it!" I exclaimed. Lauren, Bella, and I high-fived each other in the hallway. Our part of the presentation was over. It was time for Mrs. Peters and Mrs. Magee to take over and finish the lesson with our classmates.

"Wow, I think they really get it now," said Bella. "Thank you for inviting me to help you with this project."

"We couldn't have done it without you, Bella," I said.

"It's true, Bella. You were our missing piece!" said Lauren.

As we were talking, Mrs. Peters walked out of the classroom with a huge smile on her face. "You girls were terrific! I am so proud of all three of you!"

We all tried to hug her at once! "I can't believe I'm saying this, but it was actually fun to be the teacher," I said.

"When can we do it again?" asked Bella.

"Hopefully soon," replied Mrs. Peters.

Mrs. Magee stuck her head out of the classroom door and smiled. "Thank you, girls, so much for sharing your expert knowledge with us. I think everyone learned from you today, including myself."

"You're welcome," we said at the same time.

"It's time for math. Katie and Bella, will you girls come back in and take your seats? Lauren, it was so nice to meet you, and thanks again!"

"You're welcome! Bye, Katie. Bye, Bella," said

Lauren. "See you at recess."

"Bye, Lauren," Bella and I said together.

We walked back into the classroom, and everyone was clapping for us. Mrs. Strickland gave me another huge smile and the thumbs-up sign.

It was hard to concentrate during the math lesson. My mind was still busy with thoughts from the excitement of our disability presentation. I saw Adam with his hand up to answer a question on the board. He got it right and flapped. Then I saw something I've never seen before. Timmy put his hand up for Adam to high-five on his walk back to his seat. Adam's smile was enormous!

After math, we had recess. Bella, Lauren, and I were hanging out together by the swings. Olivia and Mia came over and told us we did a great job with our presentation. "At first, I thought I was going to be mad at you for making me wear that ugly hat," Olivia said. "But I won't forget what it felt like to be stared and pointed at."

"Olivia, we knew you could handle it," said

Bella. "I'm glad you raised your hand to volunteer because you were so honest with everyone about how it felt when everyone was staring and pointing at you."

"That part was rough, but it made me get it better about disabilities," said Olivia.

"Well, that was the whole point of our presentation, so I'm glad it worked!" Lauren said.

I looked up and saw Mrs. Peters talking to one of the recess teachers. The recess teacher was pointing at us, showing Mrs. Peters where we were on the playground. Mrs. Peters smiled and started walking toward us.

"Hi, Mrs. Peters," I said.

"Hi, girls. I know it's usually you coming to visit me in my office during recess, but today I am visiting you." Mrs. Peters continued, "I was just talking to Mrs. Magee. We're so proud of you girls for the lesson you taught today."

"It was a lot of fun to be a teacher," said Bella.

"Well, I'm glad to hear you say that. All of the teachers have heard about your amazing lesson. Mrs. Magee made a sign-up sheet so other teachers can request to have you girls come to their classrooms to do your presentation. Seven teachers have already signed up!"

"How do all the teachers already know about our presentation?" I asked.

"Good news travels fast," said Mrs. Peters. "By the way, your next presentation date is set for next Tuesday after recess in Lauren's class."

Just then, I heard a lot of cheering on the field. The soccer kids were out there, and someone had just scored a goal. They were all huddled around and high-fiving each other. Then I noticed that Adam was the one they were all high-fiving. He was the one who scored the goal! He was doing his best to high-five in between his happy flapping. I think it was Timmy who started the rest of the soccer kids in clapping and chanting, "ADAM! ADAM!"

Lauren, Bella, Mrs. Peters, and I all had to

high-five each other, too.

My heart felt so happy.

Things that used to be hard for me (but not anymore)

Talking in front of a large group of people

Standing up for myself

Standing up for my brother

Chapter Twenty-Two

Little Big Sister

That night at home, over dinner, I told Mom and Dad all about presentation day. Mom made my favorite meal of grilled chicken, rice pilaf, and salad. They smiled when I described Timmy trying to tell the jokes with the crackers and gum in his mouth. I think I saw tears in Mom's eyes when I explained Bella's list. They listened closely when I told them how recess was different and how the soccer kids included Adam in their game.

"Again, again, again," Michael said after I

demonstrated the chanting of Adam's name. I did it for him three times, and he smiled with his whole body.

"You really made a difference today, Katie," said Dad.

"What do you mean?" I asked.

"Well, those kids in your class really understand better about life with disabilities now. That is all because of you," he replied.

"I didn't do it alone. Lauren and Bella helped me."

"You three are a great team," said Mom.

"Thanks." I smiled.

"I am so proud of you, Katie. You're a great role model for your classmates. You taught them how to appreciate differences in people," Mom said. "It was just the lesson they needed."

Michael said, "Dessert? Dessert? Dessert?" He looked at Mom.

"Yes, Mikey, it's almost time for dessert," Mom

said.

Michael ran over to the counter and grabbed a tray. I thought he was going to drop it as he ran over to show me. "Look, Katie! Look, Katie! Look, Katie!" he exclaimed. "I made brownies for you!"

I couldn't believe it! Michael hated baking. "Really, Mikey? *You* made these?" I looked at Mom.

Mom nodded. "Mikey wanted to help me make your favorite dessert."

"Eat it, eat it, eat it!" he told me.

I took a brownie from the pan and took a small bite. "Yum, Mikey! These are good!"

He jumped and flapped. "More, Katie, eat more, more, more!"

"Thank you for making these for me, Mikey," I said.

But he had already left the room to look out the front window. I think it was Neighborhood Watch time. He needed to know which neighbors were home from work by doing a driveway car check.

"Did Mikey really help you bake these brownies, Mom?" I asked.

"He poured the water in the bowl and he helped me stir, so yes, I guess that counts as helping," she said.

I took a second bite of my brownie. "The brownies are actually really good! Maybe Mikey *doesn't* ruin everything." I smiled at Mom. "I never thought I would say this, but I'm glad Mikey is my brother. And I'm not just saying that because of the brownies!"

"Mikey is lucky to have such an awesome little sister." Mom smiled.

"Actually, Mom, I have been thinking. I am a little sister who really has to act more like a big sister. So, I am really his…"

We said it together: **"Little big sister!"**

What's RIGHT
with Mikey

Great reader

Always encourages others

When he is happy, he smiles
with his whole body

Makes awesome brownies
with Mom

He makes others smile

Acknowledgments

I would like to thank…

My husband, Greg, for supporting my dream to become a children's author and for understanding my many late nights of writing and editing.

My children, Matthew and Kathryn, for giving me the inspiration and reason to write this book and for filling my heart with so much love.

Extra thanks to my daughter, Kathryn, for her help reading chapter drafts and offering her truthful insight.

My parents, Sue and George Bashan, for their endless encouragement and love throughout every age and stage of my life—and for reading first drafts of this book.

My sister, Debbie DeBettencourt, for her support, love, friendship, and late-night editing phone calls!

Adriana Tonello, such a talented artist, for drawing the beautiful book cover that I only explained in an e-mail! Kelly Cozy, my helpful and skilled copy editor, for finalizing the editing process of the book. Sheryl Fallon, for designing the cover in a matter of moments!

My editors, writing encouragers, and dear friends: Trish Butler, Peggy Earnest, Meredith Fochetta, Niko Stanwicks, Denise Stranko, Meg Strickland and Jen Wall.

To the real Bella—for inspiring the world with her messages of hope and love.

To all of the teachers, therapists, and friends who have taught, encouraged, and supported my children on their journey, especially the outstanding faculty and staff at Nayaug Elementary School in South Glastonbury, CT.

—ABM

About the Author

Amy McCoy is a former elementary school teacher who began writing for children in the 1990s. She works for a nonprofit whose mission is to help families raising children with disabilities navigate the world of special education. She enjoys teaching yoga, exercising, spending time with her family and friends, and reading books—with and without pictures. Amy is mom to Matthew and Kathryn (the real life Michael and Katie from this story). Amy writes a blog titled *Dancing in the Rain* about parenting a child with disabilities: amybmccoy.blogspot.com

About Sibshops

Sibshops offer opportunities for brothers and sisters of children with special needs to obtain peer support within a recreational context. Sibshops acknowledge that being the brother or sister of a person with special needs is for some a good thing, for others a not-so-good thing, and for many somewhere in between. Participants in Sibshops experience activities, games, crafts, trips, and fun. To find out more about Sibshops or to locate one near you, please visit: www.siblingsupport.org/sibshops

JF
McCoy   10/16N

CPSIA information can be obtained
at www.ICGtesting.com
Printed in the USA
FSOW02n0954011016
25625FS

X